CHLOE *by* DESIGN

BACK
TO
Basics

BY MARGARET GUREVICH

ILLUSTRATIONS BY BROOKE HAGEL

STONE ARCH BOOKS
a capstone imprint

Chloe by Design is published by Stone Arch Books
A Capstone Imprint
1710 Roe Crest Drive
North Mankato, MN 56003
www.mycapstone.com

Library of Congress Cataloging-in-Publication Data

Names: Gurevich, Margaret, author. | Hagel, Brooke, illustrator. | Gurevich,
Margaret. Chloe by design. Title: Back to basics / by Margaret Gurevich ;
illustrations by Brooke Hagel.
Description: North Mankato, Minnesota : Stone Arch Books, a Capstone
imprint, 2016. | Series: Chloe by Design | Summary: Her summer
internship in New York City over, Chloe is back in Santa Cruz, now a
senior in high school and fretting over where to apply to college, and she
is having a little trouble reconnecting with her old friends — until a new
girl, Jada, suggests that Chloe and old rival Nina should design all the girls'
dresses for the winter formal dance.
Identifiers: LCCN 2016007958 | ISBN 9781496532619 (hardcover) | ISBN
9781496532657 (ebook pdf)
Subjects: LCSH: Fashion design--Juvenile fiction. | High school seniors--
Juvenile fiction. | High schools--Juvenile fiction. | Friendship--Juvenile
fiction. | Santa Cruz (Calif.)--Juvenile fiction. | CYAC: Fashion design--
Fiction. | High schools--Fiction. | Schools--Fiction. | Friendship--Fiction. |
Santa Cruz (Calif.)--Fiction.
Classification: LCC PZ7.G98146 Bac 2016 | DDC 813.6--dc23
LC record available at http://lccn.loc.gov/2016007958

Designer: Alison Thiele
Editor: Alison Deering

Artistic Elements: Shutterstock

Printed in China.
042017   010465R

Measure twice, cut once
or you won't make the cut.

Dear Diary,

This past summer was too amazing for words! Interning for Stefan Meyers in New York City was such an incredible experience. I learned so much about the fashion industry during my eight weeks there. I used to think it was all about designing, but there's so much more to it than that. I know that designing is still what I want to do, but when I have my own label one day, it'll be good that I learned the behind-the-scenes stuff too.

The only disappointing thing about the summer was that I didn't get to see nearly as much of Jake as I'd planned. I thought once I was in NYC we'd see each other all the time, but being a working girl is a lot of pressure. We're still friends and stay in touch, but now that I'm back home in Cali we see each other even less. (I know there's nothing I can do about it, but it's hard not to feel a little left out when I see Alex and her new boyfriend, Dan.)

Speaking of feeling left out . . . I've been back home for almost a month now, and I still can't seem to get back into the groove. I feel miles away from everyone else, even Alex. Everyone is talking about "college this" and "college that," and I'm still adjusting to being back. People seem to find it hard to believe that I spent two months in the FIT dorms and didn't see the campus at all, but it's the truth. My summer wasn't about touring colleges. It was about learning the fashion industry inside and out. If I could turn back time, I'd schedule a tour and learn more about FIT and Parsons when I had the chance, but it is what it is.

Another weird thing since I've been back is Nina — she's actually been *nice* to me! Well, maybe not exactly *nice*, but at least not awful like in the past. Sometimes, she'll even stop to make small talk about school and fashion. It doesn't seem like she's trying to mess with me, but it's just one more thing that makes me feel like everything changed while I was away and someone forgot to give me the new script. . . .

Xoxo — Chloe

Today will be a good day, I tell myself as I hop out of bed. I've been feeling off for too long now, and it's time to get back in the swing of things. I keep telling myself that if I just *act* happy, it's bound to rub off and make me happy for real. (So far, not much luck with that.)

I start with my outfit — cute clothes are always a good pick-me-up. I'm not in the mood for bright colors today. That means I need a fun, black dress that can hold its own. I choose a sleeveless suede shift dress in black that falls just above the knee. Its embroidered square pattern keeps it from being boring, and I can add a blazer or sweater if I get chilly. Now for the shoes. It's definitely a flats kind of day. My black sandals that lace up at the ankle are perfect.

"Liking the smile," my mom says when I arrive downstairs for breakfast. "I've missed it."

I give her a quick hug. "Me too. I know I've been kind of a grump lately. I just didn't realize how much I'd miss by being gone for two months. Not that I regret it. It's just that everyone seems to have all their college stuff figured out, and they've hung out all summer. I don't know exactly where I fit in."

Mom nods. "I get why you feel like that, but I know for a fact that Alex is thrilled to have you home. She's practically moved in since you got back. Which reminds me — I need to buy more of those Doritos she likes."

Alex *has* been over a lot. But most of those times, Dan's been with her. Which is fine, I guess. But when they're both here, it means double the college talk. If I'm being totally honest, Alex and Dan coming over as a couple would probably bother me less if I had Jake around. But that's not an option when he lives on the other side of the country.

"Are you going to talk to your advisor today?" Mom asks. "Maybe get some info on colleges and deadlines?"

I sigh. Clearly, college talk is unavoidable. "I don't even want to think about application deadlines."

Mom smiles. "You can't just pretend they don't exist. We need to figure out when and how we're going to get back to New York City so you can tour both Parsons and FIT."

"We can just tour FIT," I say. "It's always been my dream school, and it's cheaper than Parsons."

"True, but Dad and I want you to make an informed decision. We want you to see both schools. FIDM too. That's in-state and an excellent school."

My cereal has gotten soggy, and I feel my smile slipping away. Mom is right about me trying to put off college talk, but I just wish everything could be decided already. If it could be decided without my input, that would be even better. I hate feeling so overwhelmed.

"We'll have to figure out how to pay for airfare to visit FIDM too," I mumble.

"That's right." Mom kisses the top of my hair and gently lifts my chin. "We will. Your job is to keep your mind open."

"Okay," I say. I force down my cereal and head to school. Let the Monday blues begin.

* * *

"What's with the long face?" asks Alex at my locker later that morning.

Clearly, being an actress is not in my future. I can't even pretend to be perky if I'm not feeling it. "It's Monday," I reply with a shrug. I hesitate for a moment and then add, "Plus my mom decided to start off my morning by reminding me we need to tour colleges."

Alex bites her lip, like she wants to say something, and puts her hands in the pockets of her black overalls. She has the bottoms rolled up and is wearing a cute, long-sleeved striped T-shirt underneath.

Even though I've seen Alex's new look several times already, each new outfit makes me giddy. I love that she actually *likes* going shopping these days. Which is what I wish we were doing right now. Instead, I'm staring at Alex's worried face.

I sigh. "What? Spit it out."

"You really want to know?" Alex asks.

"No, but friends should be honest with each other, so speak."

"I guess I just don't think it's a bad thing that your mom brought up college tours," she says. "I looked some stuff up online, and application deadlines are in January —"

"You looked up stuff for *me?*" I interrupt.

This is so Alex. When I first heard about *Teen Design Diva* auditions — which feels like *forever* ago — I was so overwhelmed that I couldn't even look at the requirements. Alex was the one who went to the website and printed out all the information. She gave me the push and confidence I needed to apply. And don't get me wrong, I'm still super-grateful. But sometimes it takes me a while to wrap my brain around something, and my best friend's pushiness can be a little . . . well . . . pushy.

Alex blushes. "Too much? I'm sorry. I was just trying to help. You've seemed a little overwhelmed since you got back from New York. I just want you to be as excited about college stuff as I am."

I take a deep breath and count slowly to ten. I know Alex means well. But this is too much for a Monday morning. Not only do I have to make appointments for college tours and figure out paying for airfare, but this conversation has reminded me how behind in the process I actually am. I only have a few months to complete my applications and turn them in.

When I don't say anything, Alex puts her hand on my arm. "Chloe, I'll help you make a schedule. Whatever you need."

I shake my head. I don't want to think about a schedule right now. What I need is to not think. Not about this anyway.

I shrug Alex's hand away. "I need to get to class," I say. "I'll talk to you about it later."

Alex's face falls, which makes me feel even worse. I know she's trying to help, but I'm not ready for that kind of help yet.

ALEX'S OUTFIT *Design*

LONG-SLEEVED STRIPED T-SHIRT

BLACK OVERALLS

Style Evolution

ROLLED CUFFS

By the time I get home from school, all I want to do is flop down on my bed and read a fashion magazine. But the conversations I had with my mom and Alex are still running around in my mind. Maybe the only way to stop their words from invading my brain is to *do* something about it.

I open my laptop and go to FIT's website first. This seems like the best place to start. It's always been my dream school, and I'm at least *somewhat* familiar with it since I stayed in the dorms there during my internship. Maybe I didn't see anything *besides* the dorms, but it's something.

I click through the different sections on the website. The campus photos look nice, and the video showing

FIT WEBSITE *Designs*

SLEEVELESS BLOUSE & TIE

CROCHETED TOP & SHORTS

Sporty Look

JERSEY DRESS

SNEAKERS

Boho Look

Preppy Look

PLEATED SKIRT

RIBBON-TIE WEDGE SANDALS

students sketching outside makes me feel at home. The different students all seem to have their own style, which I love. It would be so boring if everyone looked the same. Some are wearing clothes that are simple and chic, like what I tend to wear. A student in a jersey dress and sneakers reminds me of Alex's sporty style. There are kids in preppier clothes too, and I admire the outfit of a girl in a pleated skirt, sleeveless white blouse, and tie. Another student is sporting a more bohemian look that makes me think of the sketches I did while people watching in NYC over the summer. The girl is wearing a crocheted top that hangs loosely over embroidered shorts, and her hair is in braids that graze the layered necklaces she's piled on.

I watch the video a little longer and then click on the *How To Apply* tab. I groan when I see I have to write an essay about why I want to attend FIT. I wish I could explain myself in clothes. It's so much easier explaining myself through my designs than through words.

With that in mind, I click on the *Portfolio Requirements* tab. The first thing on the list is another essay. My heart sinks, but I feel better when I see the topic: *Write about a hard time in a workplace.* I can handle that. My internship at Stefan Meyers definitely wasn't easy, so I'm sure I can find something to write about. The time I tried to cut corners on an assignment given to me by Laura, one of my bosses, could be a good example. Even now I shudder when I think about it. I did learn from it, though, and got another chance.

I scan the page to see what else I have to do and start to get dizzy reading through all the project descriptions. I knew I'd have to submit a portfolio of some kind, but thought it would just be a collection of my sketches. Boy, was I wrong. One part asks for samples of my designs and another wants photos of stuff I've sewn. And then there's a third task that asks applicants to create a fashion line for a pop star, imagining what he or she would wear on stage, out with friends, and lounging around.

Relax, Chloe, I tell myself, taking a deep breath. *One thing at a time. This is totally doable. You've got this.*

I print out the pages and stack the papers into a neat pile. Then I decide to take a break. That was enough for one day, right? I pick up one of my magazines and sprawl out on my bed, but I can't concentrate on the photos. A voice inside my head keeps telling me I didn't put a dent in this college thing at all. I flip through the pages of the magazine, hoping the outfits and styling tips will push the nagging voice out, but it doesn't work. I need to feel like I did *something* today.

Reluctantly, I put my magazine down and pick up an old sketchpad, flipping through until I get to the sketches I did for my *Teen Design Diva* auditions. They give me an idea, and

I run to my closet. I can use some of the designs I sewed for the auditions for my FIT portfolio. The silk dress I designed for the first round of auditions was one of my favorites, but the stitching was really off, which means I can't use it. That was before I learned how to sew silk properly.

Light-bulb moment! I can email the *Design Diva* producers and ask them for photos of the designs I made while on the show. Having a concrete place to start for one part of the portfolio makes me feel better.

I look through more sketches and see one of the outfits Alex wore when she came to see me in New York during Fashion Week. I remember how excited I felt when I first saw it. The fitted black T-shirt, distressed boyfriend jeans, and studded black flats were such a surprise from her previous fashion mantra of *sweatpants chic*.

That gives me another idea — maybe one of the sections in my portfolio can be dedicated to Alex's evolving look. After all, I've definitely influenced that, and I love sketching outfits for my best friend. I start to get more excited than nervous, and scribble down some notes on my ideas. Then I draft a quick email to the *Design Diva* judges asking about the photographs I'll need. Finally feeling somewhat accomplished, I close my laptop.

But what about the other colleges? the annoying voice in my head nags again. I shoo it away. So what that I don't have a pop star picked out yet? So what if I haven't looked at the requirements for Parsons and FIDM? I can probably use the same sketches for all three applications. I'm not going to think about that now. Instead, I text Jake about my afternoon accomplishments.

My phone pings almost immediately with a message back from him: *Congrats on starting the maddening process!*

I smile. Jake always gets me. It *is* a crazy process. I decide to reward my hard work with some uninterrupted magazine reading. This is what fashion should be — fun and stress-free.

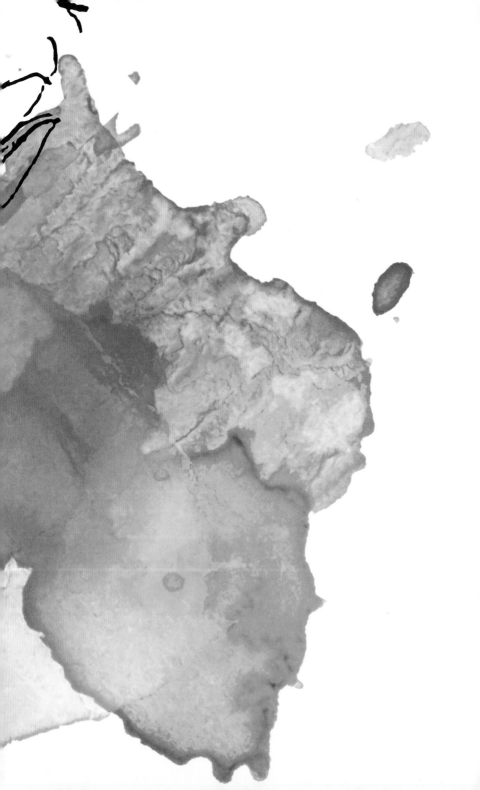

3

"So we're all getting a table together for this weekend's fashion show, right?" Alex asks at lunch the next day. We're sitting together with Dan, Alex's boyfriend, plus a couple of her new friends, Jada Williams and Mia Sanchez.

That morning, I told her about yesterday's successful college research. Sometimes I just need that extra nudge to get things started. To Alex's credit, she was all kinds of supportive and didn't say anything about the fact that I only looked up one college.

I didn't say anything about her new style being part of my portfolio yet. I want to surprise her and also not make her feel self-conscious about the clothes she chooses. Today she's wearing broken-in boyfriend jeans, a denim shirt, and leopard-print flats. I make a note to sketch it when I get home.

"Is that this weekend?" I ask. I remember Alex talking about the charity fashion show when I first came back from New York, but truthfully, I'd forgotten all about it.

Alex nods. "Yeah, it's going to showcase designs for Winter Formal."

Maybe that's why I put it out of my mind. Formals involve dates. Who knows if I'll have one? Jake might have finals that week or be busy. Or just not be able to fly here. His dad lives in California, but that doesn't mean he can fly back from New York whenever he wants. I haven't mentioned Winter Formal in any of our texts. Probably because I don't want to hear his answer if it's no.

Jada laughs. "It's probably not much compared to the New York fashion scene. But apparently, it's a pretty big deal here."

I cringe. I didn't mean to make it sound like I'm too good for the stuff here. "I didn't mean —"

"Relax," says Jada with a laugh. "I'm just kidding."

"Chloe takes things a little seriously sometimes," says Alex. "But that's why I love her." She gives me a hug. "We balance each other out."

That makes me feel better, but not understanding Jada's sense of humor is just another thing that makes me feel left out. Jada moved here over the summer from Connecticut. She seems really nice, but it was weird coming home and seeing Alex with a new friend I'd never met. She never even mentioned her when I was in New York. It's hard not to feel a little jealous when they talk about all the fun stuff they did over the summer or laugh at inside jokes I don't get. I know I'm the one who left for the summer, but sometimes it feels like Alex is the one leaving me behind.

At least Jada and I have completely different styles. I'd feel even worse if Alex had found a total Chloe replacement, but Jada has her own East Coast thing going on. Her clothes are all pretty preppy, similar to the girl I noticed in the FIT video. Preppy always makes me think serious and buttoned-up, but Jada's personality is the opposite of her style. She finds humor in just about everything. Today she's wearing an argyle sweater vest over a short-sleeved blue shirt dress. It screams Ivy League. That's good since Cornell, Princeton, and Yale are Jada's top choices. (Believe me, I've heard all about it.)

"A table would be great," I say. "Any word on the styles they're showcasing?"

"Nope," says Mia. "But I'm hoping for something a little out there and crazy."

I've hung out with Mia before, but she and Alex became really close over the summer. Mia's style is more edgy than mine. Today, she's wearing a V-neck tie-dyed sweater with bell sleeves over a distressed denim skirt.

CM

STUDENT
DEVELOPMENT
Sketches

JADA'S
PREPPY STYLE

LIGHT
DENIM
SHIRT

ARGYLE
SWEATER
VEST

DARK
DENIM
JEANS

ALEX'S
NEW STYLE

BLUE
SHIRT
DRESS

TALL
BLACK
BOOTS

LEOPARD-
PRINT
FLATS

The tips of her dark hair are dyed pink. I've seen them blue and green too.

Dan, Alex's boyfriend, takes a bite of his sandwich. "The parents are running the show, so I wouldn't hold my breath."

"Not like you'd care," says Alex. "You're lucky. You just wear a suit and call it a day. A shirt with color would be wild and crazy for you."

"That is correct," says Dan. "I'm a no-frills kind of guy."

"And that's why you're so awesome," Alex says, taking his hand.

Just then my phone pings, saving me from further Alex-Dan mushiness. It's an email from one of the *Design Diva* producers with photos of all the designs I did for the show. They sent photos of everything I ever made, including my audition stuff. How sweet! I feel myself getting sentimental and pull myself together. But not fast enough.

"What's up?" Alex asks, separating herself from Dan long enough to peer at my phone.

"Just one of the producers from *Design Diva*." I show her the photos. "I emailed to get photos of the pieces I made."

"Nice! That'll help with the college application stuff, for sure."

"I can't wait until that's finished," Jada says, overhearing Alex's comment. And just like that we're off the fashion show topic and onto college talk again. "I'm applying early decision, so it's going to be crazy until the November deadline, but then I'm home free."

"Ugh!" Mia says. "I'd die if I had to submit stuff that early. But at least I don't have to make a bunch of different portfolios like Chloe. I so feel for you, girl."

"What do you mean?" I say. Clearly Mia doesn't know what she's talking about. "I'm planning to use the same designs and portfolio for all the schools."

Mia shakes her head. "My older sister is at FIDM, and she had to have different sketches for every school she applied to," she says, oblivious to Alex waving her hands in the air. Finally, Mia notices. "What are you doing? Is there a fly?"

I slump down in my chair. "No, Alex just knows all this college stuff is kind of freaking me out, and she wanted me to live in my happy place a little longer. It's just a little overwhelming."

Mia frowns. "Sorry, Chloe. I figured you already knew. My sister had all kinds of designs. I think one was amusement-park themed. I can ask her, if you want."

"No," I say weakly. "That's okay. Don't ask."

"You sure?" Mia takes out her phone, ready to call.

I nod and put my head in my hands. Just yesterday I was feeling terrific about my progress. Now, I see I have so much more to do. When I get home, I just want to crawl under the covers and not think about all the work ahead of me.

"So, back to the fashion show," says Dan, changing the subject, even though I know he couldn't care less about the show.

"Right," says Jada, picking up on his cue. "I'm hoping for some sleek evening dresses. Something classy."

"Chloe?" Alex says, trying to draw me in to the conversation. "How about you? What are you thinking?"

I barely hear her. All I'm thinking about are the portfolio requirements I have no interest in looking up. And an imaginary pop star whose wardrobe I need to create.

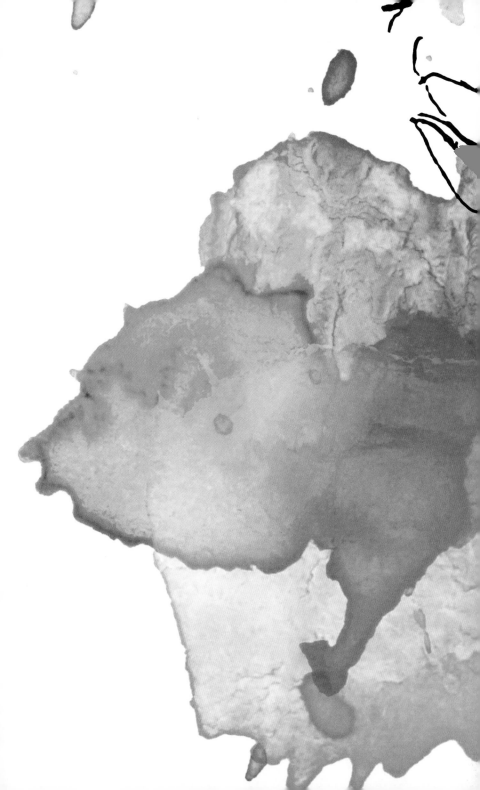

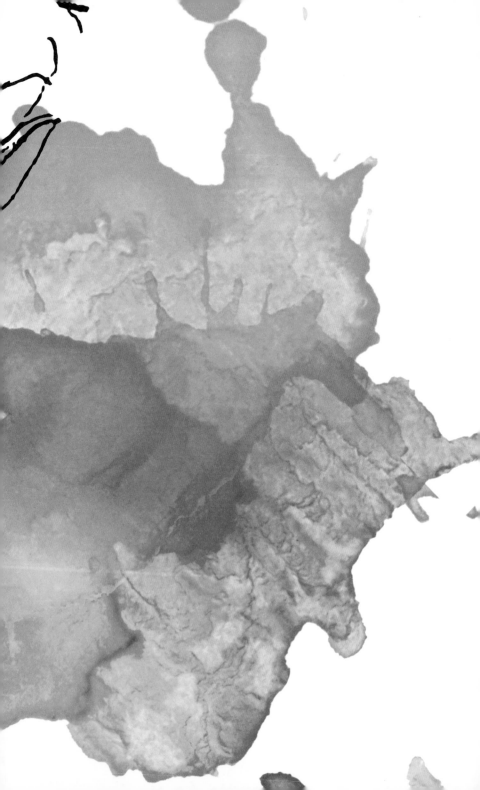

By Saturday, the school gym has been transformed into fashion central. You can barely tell it was ever a gym. Tables have been set up on one side, and the floor is covered in a shimmery white fabric. A stage and speakers have been placed at the front of the room, and lights surround the runway. I had my doubts about what kind of fashion show the school could pull off, but it honestly doesn't look that different from the shows in New York City.

"Wow! This is so impressive," I say to Alex when we arrive.

"I know! I didn't expect that at all," she agrees. "It reminds me of the runways in New York from when I came to visit."

We share a smile, remembering our time together at Stefan's Fashion Week show, and I feel more in my zone than I have in weeks. I feel like Alex and I are connected, like we have our own special relationship the others don't. The fact that we're at a fashion show puts me more in my element too. For the first time in a long time, I don't feel left out.

I catch a glimpse of Nina behind the stage helping the models with some alterations and walk over. For a second, I wish I'd come back from New York sooner. Then I could be helping at the show too. But the thought quickly passes. Today, I'm glad I get to relax with my friends and not deal with the runway angst.

Alex sees some friends at a nearby table and makes her way over while I duck backstage to say hi to Nina. I'm trying to be nice because she's been civil lately. And, like it or not, Nina and I probably have the most in common when it comes to college applications.

"Hey," I say to Nina. "How's it going? Staying sane back here? Fashion shows are a lot of work."

Nina shoots me an unreadable look. "I'm sure this doesn't compare to New York, but I'm doing what I can." Her tone is a little snippy, which could be because she's stressed with last-minute details or because she thinks I've come to brag — knowing Nina, probably a little of both.

"Actually, this set-up is really amazing," I say.

Nina pauses mid-pin and glances my way. "You're not being sarcastic?"

"Nope."

Nina looks confused for a minute, but then forces a smile. "Thanks."

"Sure. Good luck."

"Where'd you disappear to?" Alex asks when I sit back down at our table.

"I just ducked backstage to say hi to Nina and see how things are going," I reply.

"Nina? You and Nina were actually having a pleasant conversation?" Alex says, looking shocked.

I shrug. "Seems like. You have to admit she's been nicer this year since I got back. Maybe she's finally decided to bury the hatchet since it's senior year."

"Hmm . . . well, I don't know," Alex replies. "I still wouldn't trust her."

"We're not sharing clothes or anything just yet, but . . ." I want to say I have a feeling that Nina will understand how anxious I am about all the portfolio stuff, but I know that will make Alex feel like I'm somehow saying she *doesn't* get it.

"A fashionista doesn't change her polka dots that easily," Alex says, letting me off the hook. "That's all I'm saying."

I laugh. "Look at you trying to make a fashion analogy. That's so cute."

Alex gives me a playful shove.

"What's cute?" Jada asks just then as she and Mia arrive and grab seats at our table.

"Alex being fashion-y," I say.

Mia grins. "It does take a little getting used to," she says.

Jada looks confused. "I'm missing something, right?"

Alex blushes. "Well, let's just say that before this past summer I wasn't the put-together fashion icon you see before you." She gets out of her chair and pretends to strut down an imaginary catwalk to show off this evening's style: a black short-sleeved sweater, blue jeans with the cuffs rolled up, and chunky black sandals.

We all crack up, and Alex makes her way back to her seat. Just then, the lights dim and the music starts. I immediately snap to attention.

This is where I belong.

ALEX'S OUTFIT *Design*

SHORT-SLEEVED SWEATER

Style Evolution

CHUNKY SANDALS

ROLLED DENIM JEANS

5

Everyone focuses on the runway, and a moment later, the model walks out in a green A-line dress that falls to her knees. The waist is cinched, and the sleeves are poufy. It reminds me of the party dresses Alex and I loved when we were little kids. The dress has potential, but I wouldn't wear it as is. It's a little too young and wholesome.

I take out my sketchpad and draw the design on the runway on one side, then imagine how I'd change it on the other. I make the hemline asymmetrical, so it's shorter in the front than the back. I also change the sleeves from poufy to fluted. This way, they start off fitted but then flare out by the wrists. They would look pretty in a sheer material too.

Alex leans over and peeks at my drawing. "That's beautiful," she whispers. "I would so wear that."

As the show continues, I keep one eye on the runway and the other on my sketchpad. I try to capture the dresses I love, as well as the ones I'd tweak to better fit my style.

Lola James's new song — about life in New York — floods the speakers, and I take that as a sign and doodle, *New York + fashion = Chloe's favorite things* across a new page of my sketchpad. Before I realize what I'm doing, I'm using Lola James as my model and drawing my Winter Formal designs on her.

Then it hits me — she can be my pop star for my portfolio! She's one of my favorite singers, and her songs are the perfect inspiration too — they'll give me plenty of ideas for outfits she'd wear out with friends, to red carpet events, or when she's just chilling on the couch writing music.

Brightly colored dresses fill the runway, and I add them to my sketchbook, changing some so that the colors act as accents rather than the majority of each dress. I change the backs too. I draw crisscross straps made of rhinestones on one sketch. On another I change the back design to a scoop back.

Remembering the art deco-inspired work I did for Laura and Taylor during my internship, I spice up some designs with embellishments. One dress gets a beaded bodice, while another gets a V-neck studded with crystals.

By the time the fashion show draws to a close an hour later, I have more than ten pages of sketches, my pop star picked out, and a new attitude.

* * *

"That was really fun," says Jada after the models do their final walk on the runway. "It must have taken a lot of work to put it all together."

"You have no idea," says a voice behind me.

I turn around and see Nina standing there. "You should be proud," I tell her.

"I am, but those designs . . ." she trails off and frowns.

"They were kind of lame, right?" says Mia. "No offense."

"None taken," says Nina. "The parents in charge had a very specific vision of what they wanted. They didn't really care when I tried to say we wouldn't wear most of those styles."

Alex clears her throat. "Chloe did some really amazing sketches during the show."

"Yeah?" says Jada. "Can we see?"

I shyly open my sketchbook and show them my designs. "They're just doodles," I mumble. "The full sketch will look way better."

SCHOOL FASHION SHOW Designs

Original Look

New Look!

POUF SLEEVES

FLUTED SLEEVES

HIGH-LOW SKIRT

A-LINE DRESS

"Stop," says Mia. "These are fantastic. I'd wear any of those."

"Same here," says Jada.

Nina pushes her way in beside Mia to get a better look. "They *are* good," she says grudgingly. "Not exactly *my* style but nice."

Alex snorts and gives me an I-told-you-so look. "What exactly is *your* style?" she asks.

"Something a little more feminine and refined," says Nina. That vision matches with the long-sleeved floral romper she's wearing.

"You know," says Jada, "I have a great idea. What if Chloe and Nina designed our Winter Formal dresses?"

"That would be awesome!" Mia agrees. "I bet lots of girls would be into that."

"Together?" Nina says, shooting me a slightly panicked look. "I don't —"

I'm all for designing dresses . . . but not with Nina. It's one thing that we're not mortal enemies anymore. But it's another to work together, especially when we have such different design styles.

"Yeah," I chime in. "I don't think that would work. Nina said her vision is different from mine and —"

"Relax, you two," Jada interrupts. "I bet there are girls whose tastes lean more toward Nina's and others who'd prefer Chloe's vision. Besides, it will be a lot of work. No way can one of you handle it all."

"I can handle a lot," Nina mutters.

I shoot her a look. "Me too," I say. After all, I've designed stuff that went down the runway during Fashion Week. I can definitely handle a few dresses for Santa Cruz's Winter Formal.

"Okay, then," says Alex. "It's decided. Let's start spreading the word."

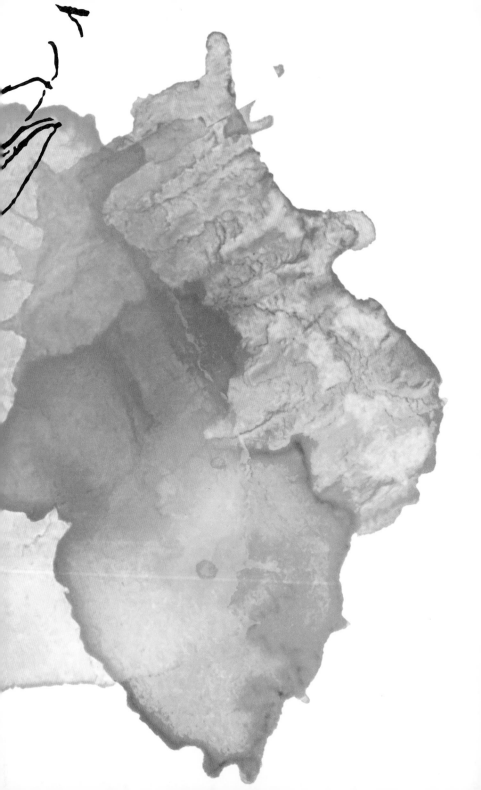

6

A week later, my room looks like a tornado went through it. My floor is covered with sketches, fabric samples, and containers filled with embellishments. Since Nina and I agreed to design dresses for Winter Formal, I've had appointments almost every day. My parents have been really supportive, but when two girls showed up during dinner a few days ago, they drew the line. From now on, I'm not allowed to have more than one appointment per day. On weekends, I can have more as long as they don't interfere with dinner or family plans.

I enlisted Alex's help in making a schedule, and she was thrilled. She loves organization and was so excited to keep track of the materials used and scheduling appointments. She even offered to keep track of any input Mimi — my favorite local boutique owner — provided. Nina and I realized that we didn't have time to design the dresses *and* make them, so Mimi graciously offered to help with the sewing.

"This will look amazing on my college applications!" Alex exclaimed when I asked. "What school wouldn't want a future business major who's already doing business stuff in high school?"

That got me thinking — not only can I make my Winter Formal designs part of my portfolio, this could also be the start of my own label. Don't get me wrong — that's a *big* jump, and I know it. I mean, I'm confident in my designing, but starting my own label is a lot of pressure. But it's what I want more than anything else. So I'm trying to be positive and not typical Chloe who doubts herself at too many turns.

"Who's next on our list?" I ask Alex when she shows up for our Saturday afternoon appointment.

Alex pulls out her laptop and pulls up a spreadsheet she made. "Sophia Gonzalez. Do you know her?"

"I've seen her around. She's in the animal rights club, and she played Glinda the Good Witch in *The Wizard of Oz* last year. I think she has pretty girly, feminine style."

Alex makes a face when I say the word *girly*, as if there's nothing worse than that.

I roll my eyes. "Girly can be really pretty. I can work with that."

Just then, my mom knocks on my bedroom door. "Your next client is here," she says very seriously. She can be really silly sometimes, but I do like the sound of that. It's like I'm running a real business.

"Hi, Chloe!" Sophia says, walking into my room. She's wearing floral pants and a lacy, off-the-shoulder blouse. Her hair is swept up with a lace ribbon. "Thanks for squeezing me in. I'm so excited about this! It's going to be so cool to have a custom dress! I even brought some designs."

"Very cool," I say, taking the papers from her hand. "It's really helpful if I have a clear idea of what you want."

"I actually showed these to Nina first," Sophia says, "but she said you might be a better fit."

"I'll bet she did," Alex mutters under her breath.

I shoot Alex a look that says *zip it* and then turn back to Sophia. "I'm sure I can come up with something based on these. Why don't you have a seat while I look through them, okay?"

The fact that Nina sent Sophia here gives me a bad feeling, but I try to shrug it off and look at the papers — photos from magazines pasted together with some of Sophia's ideas drawn in — with an open mind. I do this kind of thing when brainstorming too, but as I flip

SOPHIA'S INSPIRATION *Sketches*

CINDERELLA-TYPE BALL GOWN

TULLE

SEQUINS

FULL SKIRT

OFF THE SHOULDER

BIG BOW

DROP WAIST

through Sophia's ideas, I realize there's a major difference. The designs I pick go together. These don't — at all.

One page shows a Cinderella-type ball gown bottom paired with a sequined top, and Sophia had added poufy sleeves similar to what we saw at the fashion show last week. Another combination is a skirt with layers of tulle and an off-the-shoulder, high-necked velvet top. I see more and more mismatched combinations as I flip through the stack. I like an element of each design, but the way Sophia seems to envision them together is a little bizarre.

I feel Sophia's eyes on me and force myself to smile. There's more to being a fashion designer than just drawing. I have to learn to sell my ideas to clients too, or there's no way I'll make it as a designer. I take a deep breath. Here goes nothing.

7

"You have a lot of great ideas," I start, hoping I'm being tactful. I rack my brain, trying to figure out how to phrase the next part so it doesn't hurt her feelings. I know how crushing it can be to present an idea you think is terrific, only to be told it won't work at all — I had plenty of experience with that during *Design Diva* and my internship. I tap my pencil on my lip. "A lot of great ideas," I repeat to give myself more time to think.

I remember how helpful it was when the *Design Diva* judges or my internship supervisors told me how to fix my designs but also emphasized what was good about them. The positive stuff gave me confidence and made me feel less hopeless about the things I had to fix.

Alex snorts beside me, and I give her a stern look. She pretends to study her spreadsheet.

Sophia looks at me expectantly. "So, the thing is," I begin, "I'm not sure how some of these designs fit together." Sophia's face falls, and I rush to say something promising. "But, I think it's just a matter of moving some things around. There's definitely stuff here I can use."

Sophia perks up. "Great! I mean, it doesn't have to look *exactly* like it does in my pictures. I'm open to input. Kind of."

I look at the designs again. "Maybe the best place to start is by you telling me which styles are your absolute favorites. Then, we'll go from there."

I hand Sophia her designs, and Alex gives me a thumbs-up as Sophia scans her drawings.

About ten minutes later, Sophia has circled a few styles on each page. "I really like a fairy-tale princess type of look," says Sophia, blushing. "Something you'd see in Disney movies. Is that too silly?"

This sparks something for me. I have the perfect Disney princess in mind, and it's a perfect fit for Winter Formal. "Not silly at all! Actually, you gave me an idea. One sec."

I draw a very rough sketch of a strapless ice-blue gown. I also add a belt in a slightly darker shade of blue to create some contrast and define the waist. When I'm done sketching, I show my picture to Sophia, and she gasps.

"Is that a good gasp?" I ask.

"Definitely!" says Sophia. "I love this skirt. It looks like a ball gown."

"Yay! That's what I was going for. Now for the top. What kind of neckline would you like? You can do a sweetheart. That would look pretty." I make a slight alteration to the sketch to show her what I mean.

"It would," says Sophia, "but I'm not totally sold on strapless to be honest. I don't want to be pulling my dress up all night. And is there any way to add lace?"

I stifle a sigh. After all, the client is always right — at least that's what they say. Instead, I focus on my sketch and add straps and a scoop neck, covering the bodice of the dress with lace.

"Wait," says Sophia. "Maybe not lace. Beading?"

This time I can't help it — a small sigh sneaks out. But I turn back to the page and add beading along the neckline. I use a colored pencil to add shades of gold and silver. It looks like a covering of snowflakes.

"Oh, that's pretty!" Sophia says, peering at the sketch. "But wait — maybe beading isn't right. Maybe sequins?"

I take a deep breath, and Alex types hard on her laptop.

"Um, Alex, would you mind getting me a glass of water, please?" I'm afraid if she stays here longer she'll snipe at Sophia for being so indecisive.

"Gladly," says Alex, looking relieved.

"Sorry," Sophia says to me when Alex is gone. "It's like I see it in my head but can't exactly explain it. Has that ever happened to you?"

"All the time," I say. I think for a few minutes, trying to mentally piece together all the different elements Sophia has mentioned. "Okay, I think you'll like this."

I flip to a clean page in my sketchbook, and get to work. I keep the basic silhouette of the dress the same but add sleeves and a higher neckline, making them both sheer — I'll have Mimi use illusion netting for that. I keep the fuller skirt, but change it to tulle. Then I add tons of crystal and floral appliques to the top and midsection, thinning them out near the bottom, turning the dress into a shimmery winter wonderland of a design.

When I'm done, I show Sophia the sketch. Her eyes light up. "This is exactly what I was thinking. No, it's much better than what I was thinking. Thank you!"

I smile, relieved that I finally nailed it and happy to have a happy client. "I'll make a copy of this for Mimi. Here's her number. Call her to arrange a fitting for your measurements."

"Thank you so much, Chloe," Sophia says as Alex walks back in. "I'll be sure to thank Nina for sending me to you."

"Don't worry," I say, smiling. I can't wait to see the look on Nina's face when I tell her how fun it was designing Sophia's dress. "I'll be sure to tell her myself."

SOPHIA'S DRESS IDEA *Sketches*

SWEETHEART NECKLINE

SKINNY STRAPS & SCOOP NECK

- *Icy*
- *Sweet*
- *Sheer*

BEADED NECKLINE

LACE-COVERED BODICE

SHEER SLEEVES

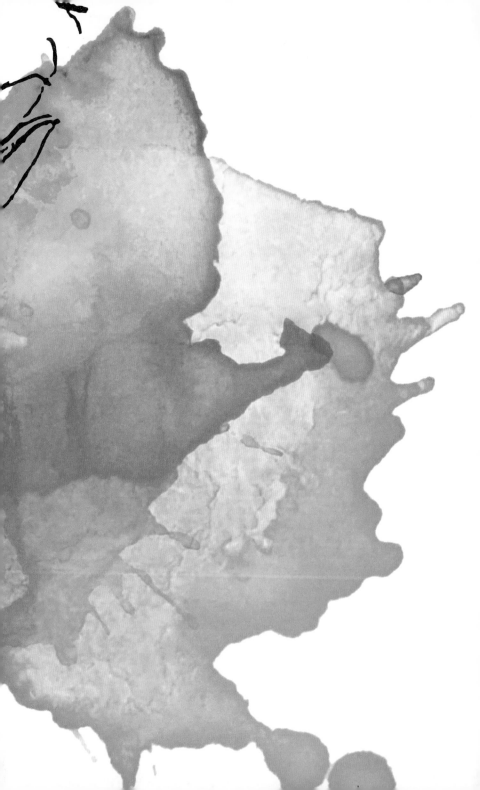

The next day, as promised, I head over to Mimi's Thrifty Threads to drop off the sketch for Sophia's dress. Mimi's store has the power to make everything better. It always has. It was my refuge even before my *Design Diva* days. There's just something about it that feels warm and welcoming.

I wave to Mimi as I walk in and busy myself by looking at the clothing on the racks while she helps the last customer of the day. Right away I spot several new designs, like a silk blouse with a suede collar. There's another blouse with the materials in reverse — suede shirt and silk collar. After working on collars during my internship, I notice them a lot more than I used to.

I've always admired the risks Mimi takes in her designs. She's never been afraid to experiment with colors or patterns. She says it's from her time working as a designer and seamstress in New York City. It made her open to a range of styles and people's tastes. Today, for example, she's wearing a bright orange blouse, black leggings with thigh-high boots, and a large belt with a gold clasp in the middle. She has her hair pulled back with an orange and gold scarf.

I'm lost in thought, thinking about my internship, my portfolio, and the Winter Formal designs when Mimi walks over. "What did you bring me today?" she asks.

"Another design for Winter Formal," I say, handing over the copy of the sketch I made.

"It's very pretty," says Mimi, looking it over. "What kind of fabric were you thinking?"

"Probably tulle for the skirt, illusion netting to cover the bodice and sleeves, and then lots of beading. I really want the illusion netting to act as a base for the embellishments more than anything else."

"Got it," Mimi says, making a few notes on the sketch. "So now that that's done, what else is on your mind?"

I laugh. "How do you know something is on my mind?"

Mimi gives me a knowing look. "Darling, don't be offended, but you're not that hard to read. Especially when I know you so well."

I laugh. "I guess it saves me the trouble of figuring out how to bring stuff up."

Mimi goes behind the counter and plugs in her brewing machine. Then, she pours each of us a cup of tea. Mimi's mug is shaped like a handbag, and mine is shaped like a high-heeled shoe.

"Mmm," I say. "Smells like vanilla." I take a comforting sip of my beverage. Mimi doesn't push me to talk, which I appreciate. I take another swallow of tea. "The thing is," I finally say, "I'm kind of freaking about the whole college application thing, but I'm not exactly sure why. I just can't seem to stop procrastinating and get focused. So far I've only managed to look at the portfolio requirements for FIT."

"How were those?" Mimi asks.

"Doable. I can use some of the designs I already have. And I'm planning to use Alex's evolving style as another theme. They also want a wardrobe for a pop star, and I chose Lola James," I say.

"Well, it seems like you have that application under control then."

"I guess," I say with a shrug, "but that's just one school. I'm planning to apply to Parsons and FIDM too. Oh, I almost forgot — there's an essay component too, which I hate."

Mimi waves her hand like she's swatting away my last statement. "The essay is no big deal," she assures me. "That's one thing that should be similar from school to school."

I put my chin in my hands. Mimi's words should be reassuring, but they're not. "What if the requirements for the other schools are too much? What if I won't have time to do them?"

"You won't have time if you keep worrying about them instead of starting," Mimi says. "You're a capable young woman, Chloe, but you have a bad habit of psyching yourself out time and time again. The important thing is that you get going on your other portfolios. Just rip off the Band-Aid, and get to it."

I look down at my mug, studying it silently. I want to say it's not possible — that I have too much going on and she wouldn't understand — but this conversation is feeling familiar. I was in the same mindset before the *Design Diva* competition. I was so worried I wouldn't be able to put anything together that I almost didn't audition at all. Then too, Mimi's tough love made me see I needed to stop worrying and just start.

I'm still not ready, though, so I try another stalling tactic. "Then, there's the whole issue of airfare. How can I afford to visit both New York City and LA? I feel bad asking my parents to pay for plane tickets, especially since I was just in NYC all summer."

"Have you not been keeping up with the new season of *Design Diva?*" Mimi asks.

I shrug. "Sort of. They're just taping now. It didn't air yet."

Mimi sighs. "Yes, and where is it taping?"

Suddenly I understand what she's getting at. Why didn't I think of this before? "LA! Oh, I should email the producers or the judges and see if they're planning to have me be a guest judge like last season. If they say yes, maybe I can combine that with a tour of FIDM while I'm there. I bet the show would pay to fly me to LA."

Mimi claps her hands. "There you go! Good job being proactive."

"But what if they say no?"

"Then they say no, and we think of a plan B. Stop thinking of things that can go wrong," Mimi says firmly. "You're not doing yourself any favors by thinking like that."

I finish my tea. I feel better and ready — or at least *readier* — to dive into the portfolio requirements for Parsons and FIDM. "Thanks, Mimi."

Mimi smiles at me. "You got it, kiddo. Remember, I'm always here for you. And a word of warning — don't be overwhelmed when you see everything you need to do. It's been a while since I applied, but I remember the requirements being fairly extensive. Just take a deep breath and start at the beginning. You can do it."

"Right. Band-Aid off and plunging in." I give Mimi a hug and then rush out of her store, heading home before this new take-charge attitude wears off.

9

"Mimi needs to start charging for her advice," my mom says when I run into the kitchen, full of new energy, and explain where I've been.

"We'd go broke," I say with a laugh. "Speaking of, she helped me come up with a great idea for the FIDM tour. I'm going to email the producers and judges and ask if there are any plans for me to come be a guest judge on the show this season. They're taping in LA, and —"

"FIDM is in LA," my mom finishes.

"Right."

"That would be a big help, Chloe. A really big help."

The look of relief on Mom's face makes me feel guilty. I've spent so much time obsessing over being overwhelmed that I haven't given much thought to how much college visits and applications — not to mention tuition — are going to cost my parents.

I give my mom a big hug and head to my room. I open my laptop and quickly type up an email to ask about the possibility of guest judging in LA. I re-read it a few times to make sure I'm not sounding too pushy. I don't want them to think I'm asking for a free ticket — but I'm hoping it'll work out. Fingers crossed.

Next, I take a deep breath and go to the portfolio requirements on FIDM's website. One of the tasks — to showcase five or six designs that highlight a personal style — is similar to FIT. It doesn't say it has to be *my* personal style. This means I can use the sketches I'm doing to capture Alex's evolving style.

The other requirement is different: *Pick a season, and create a fashion line for that time of year. You must create six to eight designs, ranging from everyday looks to eveningwear, that showcase your theme. Be creative.*

I read the instructions three times, trying to understand what they want. It kind of makes sense, but what season? The *everyday looks to eveningwear* line sparks something in my memory. The outfit I designed for the *Teen Design Diva* finale — the dress that won me my internship — could be worn in the daytime and in the evening. It had a removable collar and peplum. Maybe that wouldn't quite work here, but I could play around with convertible tops or change a look by adding small details, like accessories or a dressy skirt.

I open to a clean page in my sketchpad and write *FIDM* at the top, but then pause. What season should I tackle? I'm a California girl at heart, so summer makes the most sense. I doodle shorts and halter-tops on the edges of my paper as I think. Then, I play with the halter-top design by changing the thickness of the straps. I change the sketch more by adding a collar and making the top tighter and then blousy.

Hmm . . . halters can easily be played down or up. I look at my drawings and have a light-bulb moment — bathing suits! Those scream *summer* and there are so many possibilities. I could do fancy halter-tops, mismatched separates, or a cute, retro one-piece.

I do a few quick sketches so I don't forget my ideas and then plunge into the Parsons site while I'm on a roll. I'm all in now and don't want to give myself a chance to back out again.

The portfolio requirements seem pretty similar at first glance. Another essay: *Where do you see yourself after college?* That's actually kind of easy. I see myself with my own Chloe Montgomery label — a big *C* and *M* intertwined within a circle. As a parting gift when my internship ended, Stefan replaced his initials with mine on the back pocket of

FIDM INSPIRATION *Sketches*

Halter Tops & Shorts

BOW NECK TIE

RUFFLES

PATTERN

PEPLUM

COLLARS

SKORT

POLKA DOTS

SCALLOPED EDGE

CM logo on back pocket!!

a pair of jeans. It was the best gift ever and made me feel like having my initials on my own designs would be truly possible one day.

Okay, one last piece to look at. Parsons's main portfolio task is to create a line of clothing with one theme in mind. Wow! I couldn't have dreamed for a better project. This is exactly what I'm doing with the Winter Formal dresses I'm designing. They even have two themes — formalwear and winter-inspired!

I'm feeling so on top of things I can't resist sharing. I text Jake: *Got the requirements for all three schools down. I'm all in now!*

Jake texts back almost immediately. *There's no messing with you! New York better watch out.*

I smile and type, *New York, huh? Not LA?*

This time it takes a few seconds for his message to come through. He sends a picture of a smiley face that's blushing, along with this text: *Well . . . yeah. LA too. But you know what I'm hoping for . . . miss you and hope to see you soon!*

I blush and reply that I miss him too, all the while hoping that the *see you soon* part of his text is sooner rather than later.

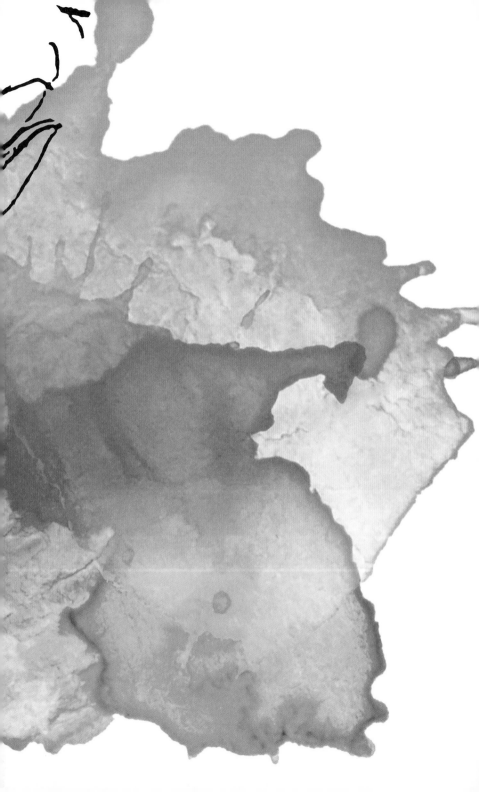

10

"You did all this yesterday?" Alex looks impressed the next afternoon when she arrives at my house, and I show her my sketchpad, as well as printouts of the portfolio requirements for Parsons and FIT.

"Yep. Jumping in. I emailed the *Design Diva* judges and producers too. I'm hoping I can combine a guest-judging opportunity with a visit to FIDM. Mimi gave me the idea."

"That's really great," says Alex. "I'm proud of you. Kick-butt Chloe, taking charge!"

"Thanks," I say. "Now, back to work. Who's our appointment today?"

Alex glances at her watch and pulls up her spreadsheet. "Tess Peltzer. She should be here any minute."

I groan. "She's kind of high maintenance. I mean, the stuff she wears to school is what I'd wear to a red carpet event. Can you imagine what she'll want for a formal dress?"

"Girls, Tess is here," my mom says just then, peeking into my room.

"Hey, ladies," Tess says, pushing open my bedroom door. She's wearing a row of bangle bracelets that go midway up her arm, lace-up metallic gold sandals, black silk shorts, and a cream top.

Alex raises her eyebrows. She and I are both in frayed denim shorts.

"Hi, Tess," I say. "Have a —"

"Here's what I'm thinking," Tess interrupts before I can even invite her to sit down. "Valentino meets flea-market."

I stare at her. Those two things are about as opposite as they get. I open my mouth to tell her that's not exactly feasible, but something tells me she won't want to hear that.

"Let's see your vision," I say instead. I was able to think of something for Sophia. I can do it again.

Tess thrusts a page from a magazine into my hands. "Something like this?" she says.

I study the image. The dress pictured *is* beautiful, but its elaborate embroidery and feathered skirt would fit in better at the Oscars than at Winter Formal. There's no way Mimi will have time to sew something like this. I study the picture to try and figure out how to tone it down so it looks like something someone in high school would wear.

"I brought this photo too," Tess says, handing me another magazine page. "It's different than what I usually wear, but it looks fun."

"Oooh!" I say. "I can definitely work with this one. I love the color." Tess's new design is more doable. The lace gives it a romantic feel, and it's more budget friendly.

Tess looks longingly at the first picture she gave me. "I think you're right," she finally says with a sigh. "The second one probably makes more sense. I've been saving up my babysitting money, but it's not enough for the feathered gown."

"Sorry," I say.

"It's fine. I know a lot of people are doing winter-themed dresses, but I want to stand out. I want something bold. Maybe red."

"Red," I repeat. "That will definitely stand out."

Tess looks pleased. "Definitely. Think of it as fire and ice. Most of the other girls will be ice, but I'll be unique as fire."

"Unique it is," I say. The goal is for the customer to be happy. And it will look pretty amazing in my portfolio. I imagine a sea of dresses in shades of blue, with the red in the middle. Scrawled across the top will be the words *Fire and Ice*. *Fire* will be in red and will look like it's ablaze, and *Ice* will be in cool blue with icicles hanging from the letters. What a great name for a fashion line!

TESS'S
DRESS IDEA
Sketch

Valentino meets flea market

GATHERED
WRAP
BODICE

FLOWER
BOW BELT

ELABORATE
EMBROIDERED
FLOWERS

FEATHERED
SKIRT

To Do List:
· *Winter Formal*

TESS'S FINAL DRESS *Design*

FIRE RED

Elegance with a "pop"

MERMAID SHAPE

LACE DETAILS

The next day at school, I'm floating on cloud nine. I'm sitting at lunch, and Mia, Jada, and Alex are all talking about how excited everyone is about my Winter Formal designs. I'm wearing a pink eyelet dress, which matches my happy, slightly blushing face.

"Don't be embarrassed, Chloe," says Mia, noticing my pink cheeks. "Enjoy the praise."

"I am enjoying it," I say. "But I'll never get used to being the center of attention."

"We'll stop complimenting you," Alex teases.

"Nah, I can handle it. Keep going," I say, making everyone laugh. Just then, my phone pings. It's an email from Jasmine, one of the *Design Diva* judges. My heart beats quickly as I open it.

Dear Chloe,

I just talked to the producers about your email and wanted to reach out. I'm so glad you wrote! Someone from the show was going to contact you, but you beat us to it. We'd love to have you come and be a guest judge. The producers are still finalizing details, but I think they're looking at Monday, a week from today. I know that's short notice, but they'll book a flight to LA, car to and from the airport, and hotel for both you and your mom as soon as you confirm.

You mentioned FIDM in your email as well. I still have a contact there and can put you in touch if you'd like to schedule a tour.

See you soon!

Jasmine

"Alex!" I say. "Check this out." I show her Jasmine's email.

"That's awesome!" says Alex. "And how cool of her to put you in touch with someone at FIDM. But whatever will you stress about now?" She gives me a wink.

"Haha," I say, but Alex is right. Sometimes it seems I'm not totally comfortable unless there's something to worry about. Maybe it's just that I need to look at a problem from all angles so I can be prepared for potential issues. Let's go with that. Over-preparedness is good, right?

"You'll need so many outfits," says Mia. She counts off on her fingers. "One for exploring LA, another for the college tour, another for judging, another . . ." Her voice trails off as she ticks off ten other outfits.

"Mia, I'll probably only be there for a few days."

"You have to be ready for anything," Mia says. I'm glad I'm not the only one who over-prepares.

"Of course," Alex agrees with faux seriousness. "You never know who you'll run into. It's LA, after all."

"That means another outfit!" says Mia. "Something for going out in LA."

"I'll be there with my mom," I remind her. "I don't think we'll be doing much going out in LA." But even as I say it, I can't help but picture an outfit that would look good among the who's who crowd of LA. Maybe something edgy, different from my usual style. I draw it on my sketchpad. Black-and-white checkered pants, gray V-neck blouse, black suede jacket, and black ankle boots.

"I love that!" Mia squeals. "I'm going to LA just so I can wear that."

"Remember everything," says Alex. "That way when I visit you there next year, I'll know what to expect."

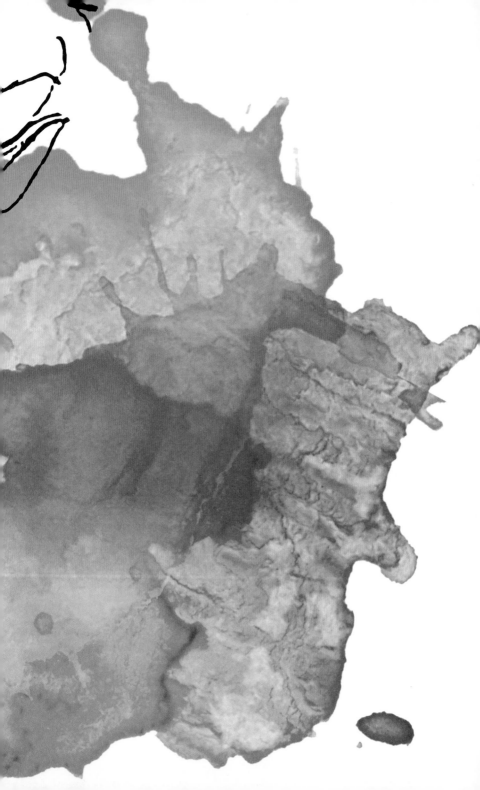

That evening, I take out my sketchpad and draw more of Alex's style for my portfolio. She's been on my brain since lunchtime. Today, she wore a black leather jacket over a white T-shirt dress and black open-toed sandals that clasped above the ankle. This time last year, those sandals would have been high-tops and the dress a baggy pair of jeans. I draw the old look beside the new one to show contrast.

I'm sketching Alex for my portfolio, but it's also a way to help me think through what she said at lunch. I know she's hoping I choose FIDM because it will be close to the California colleges she's applying to. And I'd love to be close to her too. Not hanging out with her all summer was hard, and I'm not looking forward to spending a year without her. Going to FIDM would also mean I would be closer to my

ALEX'S STYLE Designs

BLACK LEATHER JACKET

New Look

T-SHIRT

BAGGY JEANS

T-SHIRT DRESS

HIGH-TOP SNEAKERS

OPEN-TOED SANDALS

Old Look

parents. Being without them all summer wasn't easy. At least when I was filming *Design Diva*, my mom got to stay with me in New York City, but after I won and started my internship, I was flying solo.

There are a lot of things pulling me toward FIDM, I realize, but there's just something about New York City. Jake's there, of course, but it's so much more than that. Until I lived there, I never thought I'd be into the noise and crowds. I was surprised that I not only blended in, but that by the end of the internship, it felt like a second home. When I first came back to Santa Cruz, the silence was weird. For the first week, I had to play a noise app to fall asleep. It's weird that I can miss a place I only knew for a few short months.

I start to make a list of pros and cons but realize I won't be able to make a true list until I visit all the schools. FIT has always been my dream school, but that's because I didn't know that much about Parsons or FIDM. It was one of those things I decided as a kid and just went with. I'd always loved designing and had heard about all these designers who went there — people like Calvin Klein and Michael Kors. I wanted to be just like them.

But I'm seventeen now. I can't make a choice that will affect my whole life based on something I decided as a kid. Even though it would be so much easier that way.

* * *

At dinner, I feel my parents' eyes on me. I told them the good news about Jasmine's email when I got home from school, so I know they're surprised to see me being quiet.

"What's up, kid?" asks my dad. "You got such good news today. Why the long face?"

"What if I love FIDM?" I blurt out.

My mom and dad exchange confused looks. "And that would be bad because . . . ?" my mom says.

"Because it means I'd have to choose between California and New York."

"I see," my dad says slowly. "And that isn't something you thought about before?"

"I don't know," I mutter. "Kind of. Way back in my mind. But this trip makes it more real. I don't know if I can picture myself at FIDM."

"That might change once we see the campus and learn more about the school," says my mom.

"Then if it does, I'll have to pick."

My dad chuckles. "Honey, you're going to have to decide either way. Although, you could always hope they reject you. Problem solved."

My mom and I laugh. "Okay, okay. I'm worrying too much again," I say.

"You are," my mom agrees, "and I'm here to tell you that everything will be fine. No matter what happens."

"That's right," my dad agrees. "And while I won't lie and say we wouldn't love having you closer to home, you have an amazing opportunity ahead of you. We want you to choose what's best for *you*. Experience has shown us that you can handle anything thrown at you. That won't change whether you're at FIDM, FIT, or Parsons. Take everything one step at a time."

"Exactly," Mom adds. "Keep an open mind. Just think of all the great things coming up."

I give my parents a grateful smile. Their support means so much, and I know I'm lucky to have them. They're right about the opportunities I've been given. I need to focus on how it can all go right. I imagine myself on the set of *Teen Design Diva*, walking through LA, and wearing my perfect college tour outfit. There *are* great things ahead. And if I let myself experience them without any strings, there will be many more.

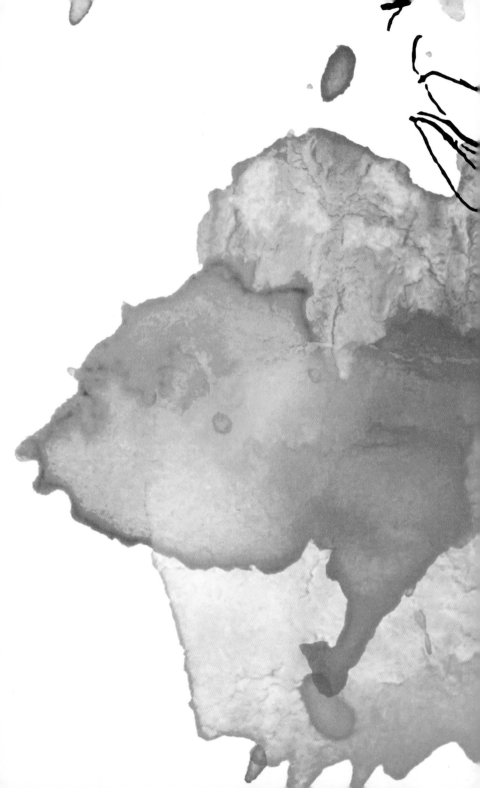

MARGIE

Author Bio

Margaret Gurevich has wanted to be a writer since second grade and has written for many magazines, including *Girls' Life*, *SELF*, and *Ladies' Home Journal*. Her first young adult novel, *Inconvenient*, was a Sydney Taylor Notable Book for Teens, and her second novel, *Pieces of Us*, garnered positive reviews from *Kirkus*, *VOYA*, and *Publishers Weekly*, which called it "painfully believable." When not writing, Margaret enjoys hiking, cooking, reading, watching too much television, and spending time with her husband and son.

BROOKE

Illustrator Bio

Brooke Hagel is a fashion illustrator based in New York City. While studying fashion design at the Fashion Institute of Technology, she began her career as an intern, working in the wardrobe department of *Sex and the City*, the design studios of Cynthia Rowley, and the production offices of *Saturday Night Live*. After graduating, Brooke began designing and styling for Hearst Magazines, contributing to *Harper's Bazaar*, *House Beautiful*, *Seventeen*, and *Esquire*. Brooke is now a successful illustrator with clients including *Vogue*, *Teen Vogue*, *InStyle*, Dior, Brian Atwood, Hugo Boss, Barbie, Gap, and Neutrogena.